Little Eight John

by Jan Wahl / illustrated by Wil Clay

LODESTAR BOOKS

Dutton/New York

for Carmen, Candice,
and Calvin Bryan
J. W.

for my mother,
Thelma Shelton
W. C.

Text copyright © 1992 by Jan Wahl

Illustrations copyright © 1992 by Wil Clay

Library of Congress Cataloging-in-Publication Data

Wahl, Jan

Little Eight John / by Jan Wahl; illustrated by Wil Clay
p. cm.
Summary: Little Eight John, as mean as mean there was, persists in
disobeying his mother until he finds his mischief backfiring on him.
ISBN 0-525-67367-9
[1. Folklore.] I. Clay, Will, ill. II. Title.
PZ8.1.W126Li 1992
398.2—dc20
[E]
91-2707
CIP
AC

Published in the United States by Lodestar Books,
an affiliate of Dutton Children's Books,
a division of Penguin Books USA Inc.,
375 Hudson Street, New York, New York 10014

Editor: Virginia Buckley   Designer: Richard Granald

Printed in Hong Kong   First Edition
10 9 8 7 6 5 4 3 2

Once there was a fine-looking boy named Little
Eight John. He looked fine. But he didn't act fine.
He was mean as mean there was.

"Don't kick at the toad frogs," his mother told him, "or you'll bring bad luck on us." But as soon as he got out of sight, Little Eight John kicked at a fat bunch of toad frogs.

The next morning the spotted cow didn't give any milk and the baby had colic. Oh my! Little Eight John just ducked his head and laughed.

"Don't sit in the chair backwards," his mother told him. "It'll bring us a mess of troubles." And of course right soon Little Eight John had to sit backwards in the wood chair.

The corn bread burned in the stove. The butter didn't churn. Oh my! Little Eight John just laughed and laughed 'cause he knew why it was.

"Don't climb trees in your best clothes." His
mother shook her finger. "It will grieve us."
So the minute he ran out in the yard, he had
to sneak up the hickory. Oh my!

And the potatoes in the back patch wouldn't grow and his father's mule wouldn't go. Little Eight John just got a fit of giggles.

"Don't count your teeth," his mother told him
one morning. "Or bad sickness may come over us."
Well sir, right then he had to go count his teeth.
He counted his uppers and he counted his lowers.

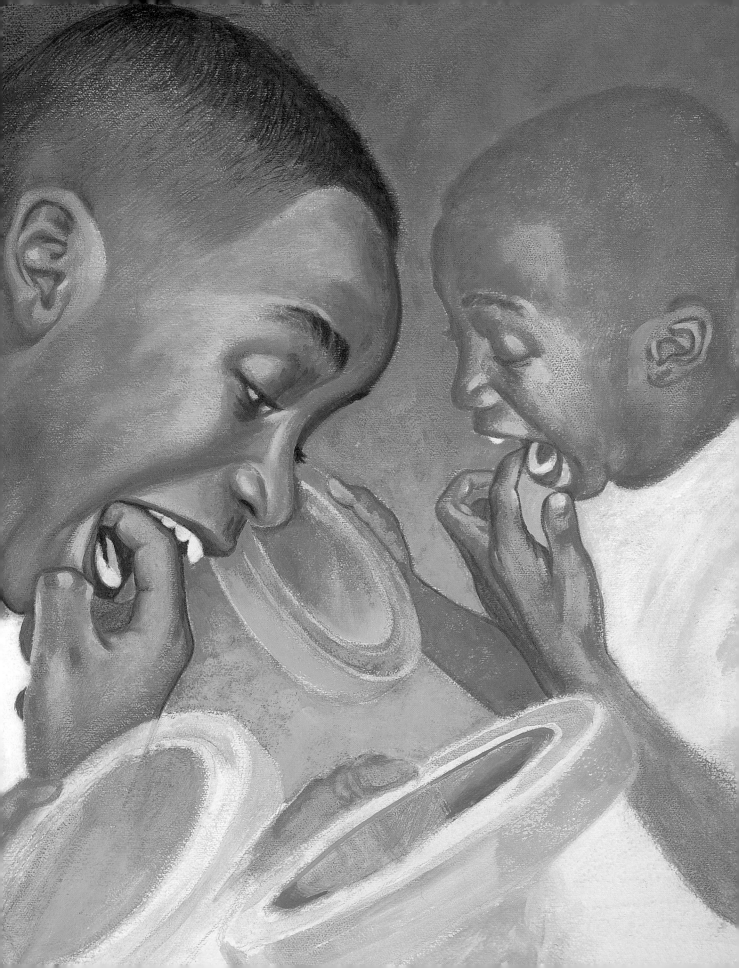

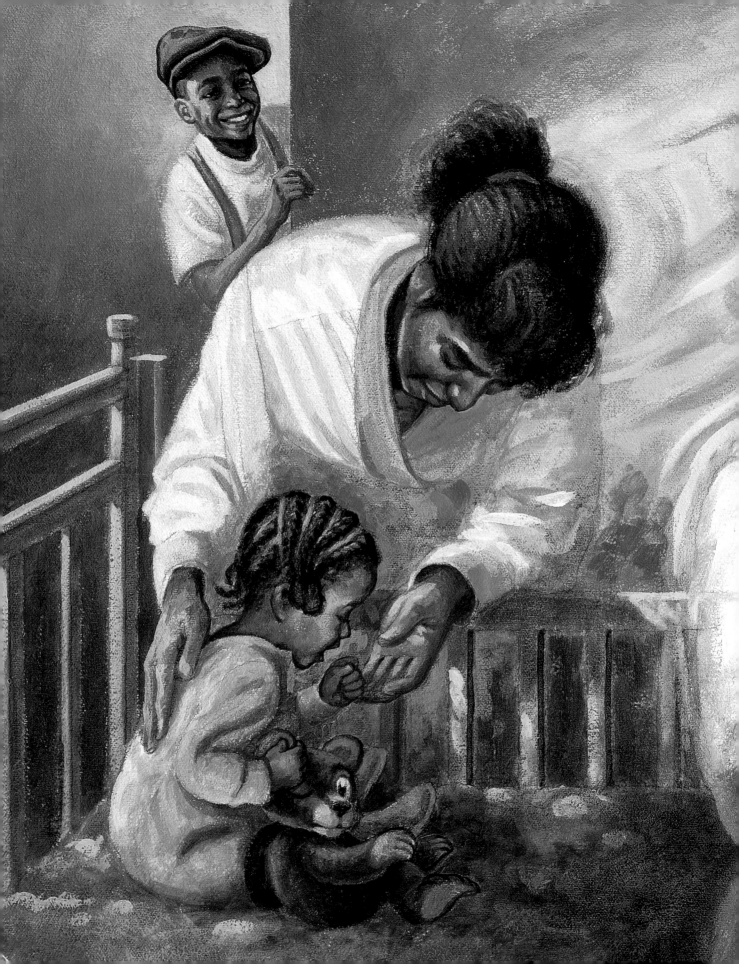

Oh my! His mother had hiccups and poor tiny
Baby got the croup. All on account of Little Eight
John and his mean ways.

"Listen, don't sleep with your head at the foot of the bed or your family will get big money blues," his mother told him.

Oh my law! That same night he slept
with his head at the foot of the bed.

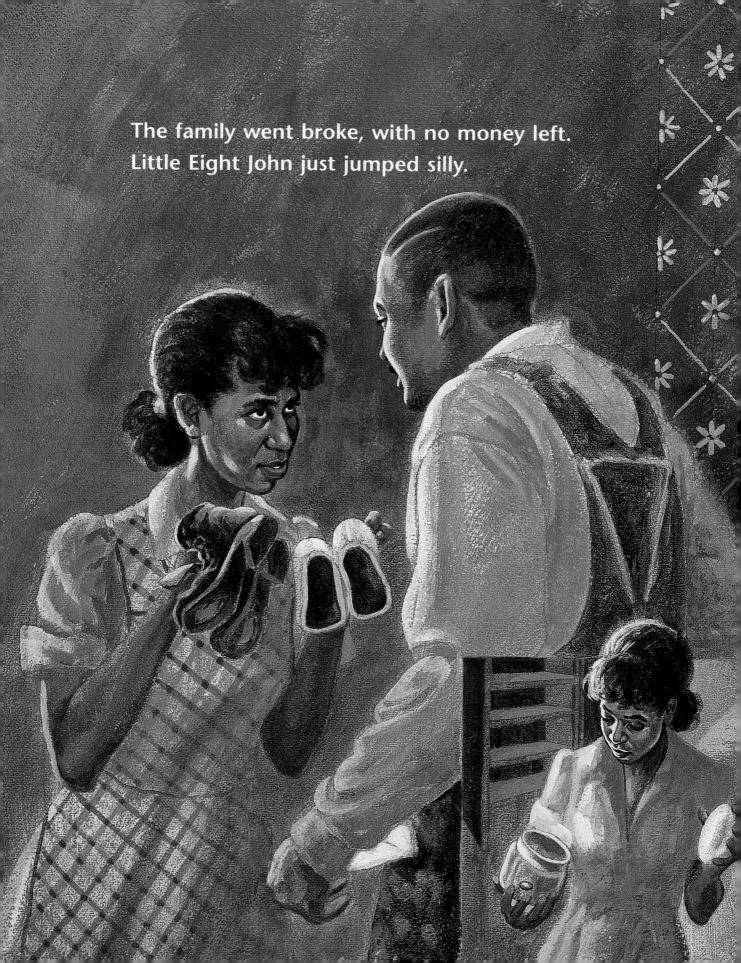

The family went broke, with no money left.
Little Eight John just jumped silly.

"Don't have the Sunday moans, for fear of Old Raw Head Bloody Bones," his mother told Little Eight John one afternoon.

Well, come Sunday he had Sunday moans and Sunday groans, and he moaned and he groaned and moaned and groaned.

And Old Raw Head Bloody Bones walked right in and changed Little Eight John to a spot of jam on the kitchen table.

His mother began to wash off the jam spot.
But before she did, Little Eight John woke up.
"Don't do it. It's me!" he shouted.

"I'm going to mind you!"
And he always did.